Golden Treads

Réka Horváth was born into an alcoholic family in 1969, in Budapest. She obtained her diploma in History and Literacy in 1993 from the University of ELTE. In 2021, she earned a Master's degree in Mental Health Studies. She has three children, and she raised her sister's two daughters, so she is a mother of five. She married in 1994 and divorced in 2023. She worked as a Marketing Director, Sales Leader, and as a Managing Director at different media companies. In 2020, during the Covid outbreak, she burnt out and she had a mental breakdown. She reflected on her past and started to heal herself.

Agnes Quirin is a graphic artist, complex art, and relaxation therapist. She finished her studies at the Hungarian Art and Design University as a Graphic artist. She got her complex art therapy diploma from John Wesley University and her relaxation and symbolic therapy diploma from Hungarian Association of Relaxation and Symboltherapy. In her earlier carrier, she created backgrounds for animated cartoons and storyboarding for animations and nature movies. She was an instructor at the Visart Artistic Academy's Advertising graphics Production department. As an art therapist, she worked with pre-schoolers, teenagers, and mothers, and she is a university lecturer in Antalfai Development and Health Promotion Art Therapy in Sapientia College of Theology of

Religious Orders. In her creations, the expressions are deeply symbolic in content as she aims to "touch the spirits within".

After graduating from a Fine Art College in Hungary, Eva moved to Canada. Her life journey was challenging and colourful. Eva attended a few different colleges and built up a carrier for herself. Some of the highlights were creating a Decorating/Painting/Renovating business and becoming an Instructor at the Vancouver School Board to teach interior design, murals, and faux paintings. She created a few three-dimensional big-scale wall murals for day-cares, baths, houses and commercial walls, etc. On the side, Eva was an accredited Interpreter/Translator across Canada, Canada Border Service Agency, and Canada Immigration and Refugee Board, and the court.

Réka Horváth and Agnes Quirin

SOARING SEAGULL AND HEAVENLY BULL

Adult Healing Tales

Translated by: Eva Csombor

AUSTIN MACAULEY PUBLISHERS™

LONDON • CAMBRIDGE • NEW YORK • SHARJAH

A CIP catalogue record for this title is available from the British Library.

ISBN 9781398494473 (Paperback)
ISBN 9781398494480 (ePub e-book)

www.austinmacauley.com

First Published 2024
Austin Macauley Publishers Ltd®
1 Canada Square
Canary Wharf
London
E14 5AA

I started to heal myself when I was 50 years old. I was introduced to and participated in an ACA (Adult Children of Alcoholics) program, which had 12 steps. This was something new and unusual for me. Some of the literature of ACA included the heavenly parents, and this vision inspired me to start the tales. Thank you for ACA!

I started to write short stories in 2020 as a healing process for myself. In my fifties, I attended a trauma writing course held by Eva Peterfy Novak, who is a Hungarian writer. Eva and the participating group members helped me to get in touch with my suppressed memories of my childhood sexual abuse. My coping mechanism was to write more and more.

Soaring Seagull

Thank you, Soaring Seagull, for coming over to see me. You are wise, understanding, and loving. I can see the Universe in your blazing brown eyes. You are my higher power, heavenly, and you came from above. I am grateful that I found you. I wasn't aware that you have been with me all the time. The little girl was dreaming about you too. The Soaring Seagull was walking with the Bull in the green meadow. The Bull was peaceful, majestic and strong. When he stomped his feet on the meadow, flowers started to bloom. The sun illuminated the Soaring Seagull's slender body. Her waist-long black braids were thrown on her chest. She had a plain white linen dress on with a belt on her waist. Her face looked young and old at the same time. Her ageless face smiled and slowly walked into the meadow barefoot. Her blazing brown eyes reflected the Universe. She walked very slowly and found the little girl in the meadow. The little girl was choking with sobs. Her tiny, skinny, bony body was covered with bruises from hitting. She was sitting and crying. She was alone. No one protected her, and no one felt sorry for her. The Soaring Seagull stepped closer to her, lifted her tearful face up, and stroked it. The stroking affected her like a healing balm. Her teary blue eyes gazed into her brown eyes. Soaring Seagull lifted her up, hugged her, and rocked her. "Love you, my sweet little one, love you," she whispered to her while still holding her in her arms. "Love you very much, you are also part of the Universe." She gently put her down, and they walked into the glowing meadow, holding hands while the sun shone upon them. The little girl was not scared of the Bull. She walked up to him and patted him. The Soaring Seagull encouraged her to sit on the back of the Bull, as the Bull was brought to protect her, to give her strength, to carry on when everything else was unbearable. Then they both sat on the back of the Bull and headed across the field into the forest between the trees. The Bull galloped along untrodden paths, but the little girl was not scared. The Soaring Seagull held her tight. The little girl saw herself in the hospital as an abandoned, crying baby. They stroked the baby and comforted her. Then they moved on. The Bull left the earth and, with a big push, leapt towards the stars. In the sparkling stars, they galloped into the endless space. The little girl marvelled at all the wonders. In this endless galloping, the Soaring Seagull whispered, "Come on, little girl, we will meet someone who loves you very much and would like to hug you and kiss you."

The Bull made a stamp in the sky and a road opened. They no longer galloped, they walked. This is where they met me, the grown-up. Quietly, tears ran from my blue eyes. The Bull harmlessly puffed. When he saw me, he pushed his moist nose towards me, asking for a pat. I kneeled down and thanked him for following me and being with me all the time. I thanked the Soaring Seagull for bringing the little girl to me. I hugged her, comforted her, and carried little Ann in my arms. All four of us continued our journey until we arrived at a clearing. The

Soaring Seagull, the little girl, and I collected some wood for making a fire. We wanted to have a fire burning for unconditional love so the little girl could warm up beside it and make the pain of shame, beating, and screaming go away. I told her that life would be beautiful, flaming, and filled with peace and love, but there would also be difficult moments and challenges. There would be sports, laughter, dancing, acceptance, and love. I had never paid attention to you, little girl. I buried you deep inside me and covered my face with a mask. I laughed or clenched my teeth to hide my pain, but my glances were like those of a hunted animal. Sometimes things felt hopeless and painful, but I patted the Bull, thanking him for the strength he provided me with. You need to know, little girl, that we will have children, we will become mothers, but our children will not have to apologise sobbingly after experiencing drunken beatings at the age of 8. They will have a protected life. But one day, my dear little girl, we will be able to live our lives by accepting who we are.

I know it was hard to bear the scars, the fear, and not knowing when and where the screams, shame, and beatings would occur. But that is all in the past now, my little one, and I thank you for surviving it. Soaring Seagull, please hug me. I allow you to guide and protect me as a grown-up. Protect me from the horrors and create peace within me so that I can believe that I have every right to this life and that I am capable of accepting who I am and loving myself for it. I know that you love me.

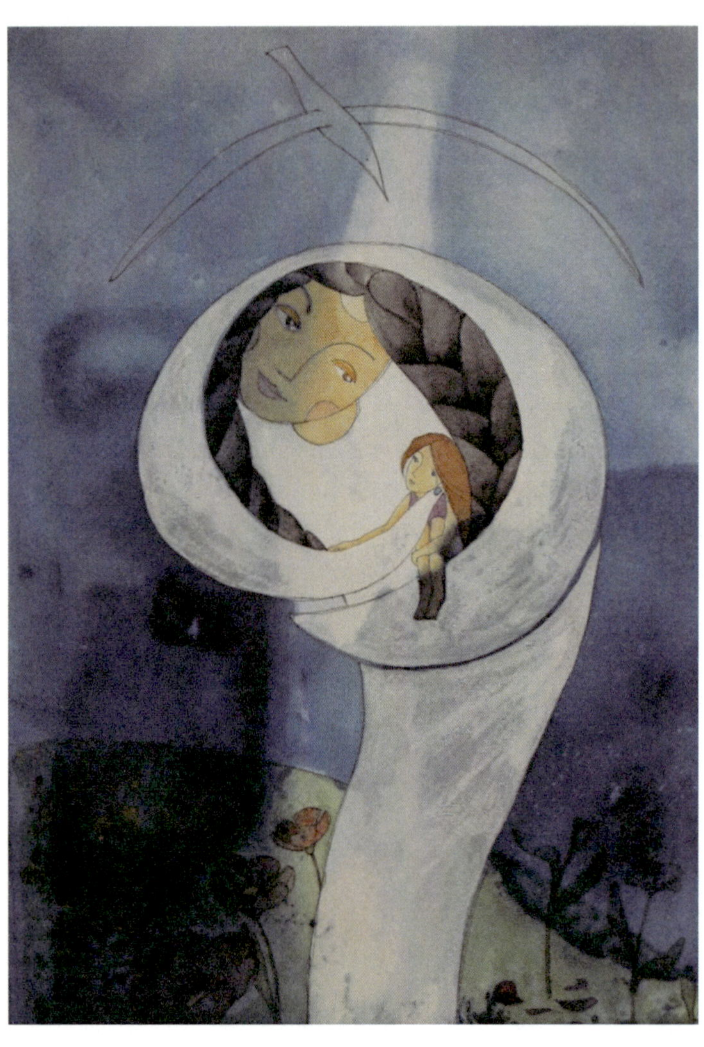

Soaring Seagull

Healing

The little girl lay on the floor. She was 10 years old, her eyes were filled with tears. The bastards pinned her down, covered her mouth with one hand, and forced her legs apart. She could feel the force enter her skinny, tiny body. She felt impaled, and crucified, and believed that her body would be torn. "If you relax, you might enjoy it." She heard a gasping voice in her ear. At this point, a Bull showed up and jumped on them. He trod and stamped on the two men to let the little girl go. Then, from the Universe, a Soaring Seagull glided by. Her blazing brown eyes were full of ferocious rage. Her timeless face shone, bringing simmering light to the little girl. She braced her, hugged her, and comforted her. The Bull kept on attacking. The little girl's body became limp and flew away. The Soaring Seagull was guarding her.

The little girl knew that the Bull's stomping did not really reach the attackers. The Bull came from a different dimension. The Bull had been there before, so she knew that the crime would stay with the attackers, and her battered, skinny body would be burned into their memory. The door slammed shut. They left.

The little girl lay on the floor, every part of her body was hurting. The Soaring Seagull hugged her and called for me as a grown-up. I appeared. We were all in the bathroom: the little girl, the Soaring Seagull, the Bull, and myself, the grown-up that she would become. We surrounded her and helped her bathe. Afterwards, we climbed onto the back of the Bull and flew up to the sky, soaring over fields and across towns. The little girl marvelled at the rooftops of houses, the church spires, and she dreamed of her own fairy tale. She saw the wonders of the world in the tall grass and among the sweetly fragrant flowers in the meadow. The Soaring Seagull gently encouraged her to whisper to the meadow what happened, to allow the grass and flowers to hold her sorrow. "Don't keep it to yourself," she said, "but let them hear your cry and let them carry it." The Soaring Seagull stroked her back as I sat beside her, and we cried together. Our tears poured uncontrollably. We had lost so much on that floor.

In the beaming sunshine, the bastards impaled our bodies and souls. I felt the presence of the Bull. "I will give you my strength and power so that you may move on, sweet little one, you will have the strength of the Bull, and my power is yours." Whispered the Soaring Seagull.

"Just cry and cry, little girl," whispered the Soaring Seagull. "The tears will heal you. You have lost a lot, but please release this memory to me so it will not hurt you anymore. I am your real mother. I will hold onto it until this grown-up person who is here is able to carry this weight. At that point, you two will unite. I must receive this, so you can move on and stay alive."

The tears poured down the little girl's face as she embraced Soaring Seagull's sleek body. "I allow you to take it away from me, I am not able to carry it." She whispered, burying her tearful face into the Soaring Seagull's embrace. I offered her words of comfort, assuring her that nothing bad could happen to her anymore. I promised her beautiful romances, the joy of giving life to many beautiful children, and the hope of one day returning to claim her as my sweet child. We had received a gift from heaven, allowing me to heal her tormented body. I pleaded with the Soaring Seagull to help and embrace us, and to restore the memory so that we could both begin the healing process under her guided protection. The Bull circled around us, and we hugged him too. Once again the four of us were together in the meadow, in pain but in peace. The little girl sat on the edge of the bathtub in the bathroom, wrapped in a towel. Her body ached, but she could not remember what had happened or why she was in pain. Then, she remembered that she had not finished mopping the floor. She completed the task, and the pain disappeared.

Healing

Healing As An Adult

Four decades later, at the end of a literacy class, a pretty brown-haired and brown-eyed girl unexpectedly told me that she was abused and raped when she was a child. She confided that she had never told this to anyone before — I was the first. As I listened to her, my heart filled with compassion and pain, and unexpectedly, the memories came back to me too. So, we were healing together, gracefully and peacefully, the older woman and the teenager — I received my gift. I survived. The Soaring Seagull and the Bull were there every step of the way, never leaving my side. Now, each night, I console the little girl with Soaring Seagull and the Bull. We play together, imagining the little girl as a child happily running around in the meadow, becoming a part of the Universe with joyous abundance. This is how her battered body and soul heal for eternity. Unconditionally, you are my true mother. Thank you for that.

Anger

By the Sea

The Soaring Seagull, who was sent by the Universe, said to the sleeping child, "Let's go, little girl." Warm light flooded from her blazing brown eyes, and her white dress illuminated the darkness. She gently awakened the little girl by stroking her forehead. The little girl stirred and snuggled up to the Soaring Seagull, recognising her as her real mother who loved her unconditionally. Then, the Bull arrived, and they embarked on the road of wonder once again. They settled on the back of the Bull and soared high into the sky amidst the starlights and moonlights. They reached the stars, where the little girl could stroke them. The sparks of the stars lit up her face. "We are going to the Sea," whispered the Soaring Seagull. "This is the Sea of Pureness. You will take a bath in it, and you can swim as much as you like. We will take care of you, and nothing bad will happen." Whispered the Soaring Seagull.

The Bull stopped at the shore. His hoofs stirred up the sand. It was sunny and warm. Beautiful trees stood on the beach, adorned with lovely flowers. The little girl was happily running around the shore. The Soaring Seagull, in her white dress, walked into the water, and the water turned white around her. She called to the little girl, "Come, dear, come into the water." The little girl happily jumped in, and her clothes fell off. The water was pleasant and white. In the water, the Soaring Seagull held her hand, and they played joyfully and in peace. After a long play, the little girl grew tired. The Soaring Seagull laid her on the sand, dried her body, and sang a lullaby to her, so she could fall asleep. "Sleep, sleep, little girl, dream about beautiful things. Sleep, sleep, little star, who is the child of the Stars and the Sea."

The little girl slept peacefully, no longer plagued by nightmares or sudden attacks from wolves. And then, I, as a grown-up, arrived. I gently stroked her fragile body, aware of the bruises inflicted upon her by predators. With teary eyes, I tenderly caressed her, knowing they broke her, and feeling her pain as he collapsed and lay on the floor. She did not remember it. The Soaring Seagull gave me a small white dress, her silence accompanied by beaming eyes. She asked me to dress the little girl in it. And now, this crushed little flower shone radiantly in her white dress.

Tears welled up in my blue eyes. The Soaring Seagull encouraged me to enter the white water, and she accompanied me. The Bull looked after the sleeping child. I swam, jumping into the water, and my dress shredded off me. The Soaring Seagull hugged me, and I felt grace.

On the shore, the Soaring Seagull presented me with a white dress. I held the sleeping little girl in my arms as we all climbed onto the back of the Bull. The Soaring Seagull positioned herself behind me. Soon we were on our way to the stars on heavenly roads.

The Bull slowed down, and we stopped. The Heavenly Gate stood open before us, and our Heavenly Father awaited. The Soaring Seagull greeted him by bowing her head. The

Bull kneeled down as I did too. I was being grateful to be there.

The Heavenly Father held the little girl's body and commanded the Angels to bring the medicine that would heal her broken body, allowing her to bear offspring, and granting her the strength to forget and live. The Angels quietly took the little girl's clothes off, leaving her naked in her deep sleep. They carefully applied a healing balm to her broken little body, to be fruitful again and be able to give life one day.

The Heavenly Father called me, the grown-up, and I was on my knees in front of him. I could not bring myself to look at him. With divine grace, he reached out to me and lifted me up. His magnificent hand touched my face, I stared at him with teary eyes and said,

"Please, please take me, I have tried so hard, in countless ways. I relied on my willpower and gave it my all, but it was not good enough — I failed. I have committed many sins, and my plans fell apart, taking me down with them." And then, the heavenly voice spoke,

"You have a lot to do. The hunting is over, so respect and love the little girl. She has survived everything, and you need to be grateful for this. Let her live, she deserves it. Now, dance freely, like a small girl. This is your dance, the eternal dance of all women. Right now, you are healing and becoming a healer. You have been granted grace, so remember that. You have a white dress on, and had a bath in the white water. The memories and the body are yours now. Do what you want. Everything comes from within. You are free. I will show you the way. Trust me and trust yourself. Pay attention to the signs. You are not blind anymore, you have awakened and will awaken others." I was on my knees once again, bowing my head, and my heart was filled with grace. I had to trust myself, as the Heavenly Father would guide me. I, who was once a violated, beaten, and humiliated little girl, and later an unfaithful wife, mother, and creator, who allowed men to freely use my body, and did not know that I had long ago lost touch with myself.

I am grateful for the grace in my life. I will pass on the healing. I have already passed on the gift of life by bearing children. I pay attention to other broken lives in the way I know best—with love and blessings. I, once a fragile, sensitive, and vulnerable woman by birth, have shed my protective shield. Now someone else is protecting me. I have been receiving gifts, and I accept them.

And one day, I will find a partner who will accept me the way I am, and I will accept him the way he is. There will be no judgement, only love, understanding, and trust, so we can be one but two people.

By the Sea

The Heavenly Amusement Park

The little girl lay in her bed, dreaming of fairy tales. She imagined that she was a hero, a prince who defeats enemies and helps people. However, she could not dream of being a princess. That dream had been lost on that floor when the monsters attacked her. She did not remember it, as the Soaring Seagull kept it hidden. The room was cold; it was winter and was freezing outside. There was no heat as they could not pay the bill. However, she learned not to pay attention to it. She had to learn to deal with it, just as she had to learn to cope with everything else.

The glowing Soaring Seagull, in the white dress, hugged and stroked the little girl like no one ever did. "Wake up, little girl." The Soaring Seagull softly whispered. The little girl snuggled up to her devotedly. Despite her cold little body, she felt cosy and warm. "Put on a nice dress, my dear," the Soaring Seagull whispered. "We are going to play at the Heavenly Amusement Park. There will be a Merry-go-round among the stars and you can imagine anything you like."

As the little girl dressed, she could hear the stomping of hoofs. The Bull had arrived. They climbed onto his back and soared up to the sky, above the rooftops of houses, farther and farther away. There was never any cold in the embrace of the

Soaring Seagull. It was always warm in there. The Bull slowed down, and they arrived at the Heavenly Gate. They heard noises, children were happily screaming. The Merry-go-round was spinning, and the little girl watched all the wonders in amazement. Everything was colourful and beaming with happiness. This was a different world, and she loved it very much. When the Soaring Seagull held her hand, she felt safe. She knew she would not get hurt, as she was with her real mother.

They stepped over the gate, and the Bull gently pocked the little girl's hand, seeking affection. She happily stroked the Bull and hugged him. It felt very good to be with him.

She then ran to the Merry-go-round and watched it with amazement. The Merry-go-round then stopped, and the little girl got in. It flew far up into the sky. She laughed and smiled, her eyes were shining. She was happy. Soaring Seagull waved at her, her blazing brown eyes radiated healing powers.

That evening, the Bull came to see me, the grown-up, who the little girl would one day become. I was crying again. My face was flooded with tears, and the pain printed more wrinkles on my face. I cried for the little girl and mourned for her tormented body, which was lost on that afternoon. The Bull pocked me, urging me to get ready as we were about to leave. I wiped away my tears and hopped onto his back. Soon, we flew up into the sky, far away towards the Heavenly Amusement Park. On the way there, the Bull whispered to me:

"The little girl is happy, soaring freely. Her real mother is guarding and protecting her. In front of the Heavenly Gate, the Soaring Seagull awaits." He said softly. There, the Soaring Seagull hugged me, and her blazing brown eyes radiated the Universe.

"Heal me too, heal me too, Soaring Seagull. It hurts too much." I pleaded, dropping to my knees. The Soaring Seagull helped me up. I faced her, her blazing brown eyes and my blue eyes were locked. She hugged me, and I felt the warmness and healing power of her body. I felt how the pain was leaving me, replaced by a growing lightness within. It was as if I had wings.

We walked towards the Merry-go-round, embracing each other. The Bull walked behind us. I saw the happily smiling little girl, as she was flying in the Merry-go-round. Her hair had rainbow stripes from the reflection of the stars.

The Merry-go-round stopped, and the happy little girl ran towards me.

"Thank you for coming over. Thank you so much for being here," she said. "Are you going to tell me my story? Will you tell me that everything is fine?" She snuggled up to me.

The Soaring Seagull embraced us, and we rocked back and forth. The Bull joined in too. All four of us were together in Heavenly Amusement Park, surrounded by all the wonders.

"Yes, my little one, I will tell you the story," she replied. "I will tell you how nice it was to be at the lake with the little boys. We were surrounded by trees, and the sun was shining. The boys were swimming in the lake and playing with balls, as I watched over them. Time stood still at that moment. They will be our strong sons."

The Heavenly Amusement Park

The Heavenly Amusement Park

In the Forest

The Soaring Seagull's slender body was beaming with light. She stepped towards the little girl in her long white dress and whispered, as she gently stroked her face, "We have to go, little girl. The Forest is waiting."

The Bull stomped in, puffing happily. He loved the forest very much. The little girl opened her eyes and snuggled into the Soaring Seagull's lap. She hugged her tight to feel the warmth of her body and bask in the beaming light.

She got dressed and sat on the back of the Bull. They were flying into the starry Milky Way, into the Universe. The Soaring Seagull hugged the little girl tightly to make her pain go away. The Bull spotted a small gap in the sky and flew towards it. The sky opened up, and the Heavenly Forest appeared. The Bull stopped at a clearing, where the birds chirped merrily. Everything around them was splendored in different shades of green, and the sweet fragrance of flowers filled the air. The little girl and the Soaring Seagull dismounted from the back of the Bull and walked hand in hand. The little girl's calloused and dry hand was hurting when the Soaring Seagull held it. The Soaring Seagull whispered to her that she should ask the Bull for help.

The little girl hugged the neck of the Bull and whispered with teary eyes,

"Help me, Bull, everything is so huge. The beddings are so big in the bathtub, I can't wring them out well with my hands and they scold me for it. I wash by hand. I am small and weak, please give me strength to carry on. Give me strength to be able to clean up the dirt, please help."

"I will give you strength, little girl," the Bull replied. "Just hug me tight." The little girl hugged him tight and felt a new strength surging inside her. Her body was beaming and shinning. She had received the gift of strength to help her endure the unbearable. She ran towards the Soaring Seagull with ease and a happy smile. The Soaring Seagull said,

"Let's go and find some healing herbs for your hands. The Heavenly Forest has the healing power." They walked together in the light, in peace, and with blessings. The bushes and trees leaned in to heal the little girl. The pain in her hands disappeared with the touch of the healing herbs and the light.

She ran around happily in the forest, her hands did not hurt anymore. She felt the forest calling her into the light, peace, and warmth to dance the Heavenly Forest dance.

The Soaring Seagull, the Bull, and the little girl danced together in the clearing. They held each other tightly, spinning and turning to the heavenly music. The little girl ran to the grass, making somersaults, handstands and cartwheels. The Soaring Seagull and the Bull watched happily how she was moving, turning, and being alive.

They all rested together, embracing the little girl tightly. She rested calmly in their warmth and shine. She was in peace. No one could hurt her, only love surrounded her.

The Bull stood up and came to get me, the Adult, to dance under the leafy boughs in the Heavenly Forest. I had a teary face when the Bull arrived, carrying the pain of the broken-up child's body still hurting on the floor. The Bull looked at me gently.

"Let's go," he called. "Soaring Seagull and the little girl are waiting for you in the Heavenly Forest." I got up on his back and we were flying up to the sky and stopped at the Heavenly Forest. The little girl happily ran towards me and hugged me.

"I will show you how I danced in the forest. How I made somersaults, handstands, and cartwheels." She was ecstatic. I hugged her very tightly.

"Show me, my little one. Let me see it." I smiled kindly.

The little girl began to dance, turning around happily, exercising in the grass in peace, love and acceptance.

I got tears in my eyes. The Soaring Seagull hugged me lovingly and spoke softly,

"Cry, cry, dear one. The Heavenly Forest will take your tears far away. Cry a lot. You did not cry then, nor later. It's time to mourn, time for the pain to come out. After that, you will have a happy smile. No worries, I will guard you."

I was sobbing in the Soaring Seagull's embrace. The pain was overtaking me, and my tears were flowing. I asked the Soaring Seagull tearfully,

"Take my pain away. I want to smile again, truly and deeply, to be happy about life. I want to enjoy the flowers and the sun."

The Soaring Seagull whispered in response,

"I will take it away, tell the Heavenly Wind to take it far away."

I felt how my body and soul got lighter, and I am soaring too. The Heavenly Forest called me to dance too. I held the little girl's hand, and we were dancing, turning, spinning, and bending in the Heavenly Forest. It was a healing dance, a grace to be alive. The Soaring Seagull and the Bull joined in, gleeful and at peace.

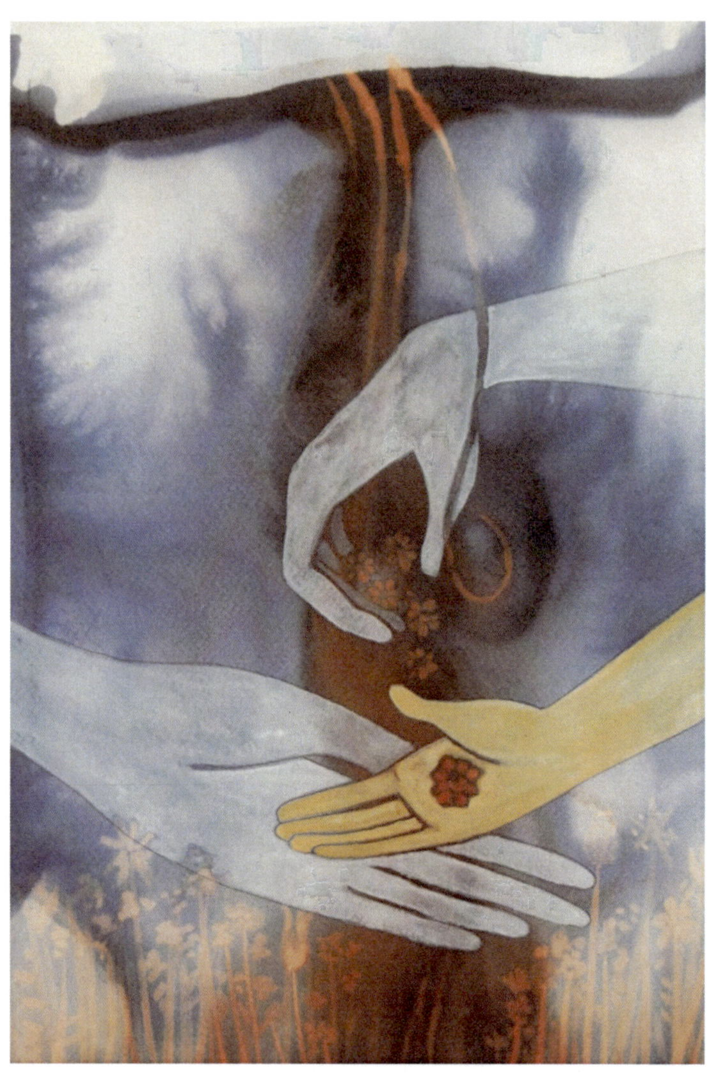

The Forest

Enchanted Mountain

The Soaring Seagull's slender body was shining as she stepped close to the bed.

"We have to go, little girl, the mountain is waiting for you." She stroked the sleeping child's hair kindly.

The little girl opened her eyes and happily hugged the Soaring Seagull. She got dressed, and by this time the Bull had arrived. The little girl hugged him. She felt peaceful and happy.

They sat at the back of the Bull, and they were ready for the heavenly journey. The little girl's tired body was relaxed in the Soaring Seagull's embrace.

They were flying up to the sky, into heavenly places reflecting the glitters of the stars and the moon. In the distance, a mountain appeared, and they were flying towards it. The Bull stopped at the foot of the mountain, and then the Soaring Seagull and the little girl got off his back.

The little girl was a bit scared and snuggled closer to the Soaring Seagull.

"This mountain is huge, and I am so little." She whispered.

"Don't be scared, little girl. I am here with you. This Enchanted Mountain hides a lot of treasure. You will find friends and helpers." The Soaring Seagull replied. As she spoke, the stones and rocks started to sing, greeting the newcomers.

The little girl was amazed by the sound of the music. Unknown beauty unfolded as the stones came to life and were glittering in endless colours. She was not scared. Happily, she walked towards the rocks, holding the Soaring Seagull's hand. The Bull followed them.

As they walked, she touched a rock, and the rock turned into a small elf. She touched more and more rocks, and they all turned into elves. There was an army of elves. The little girl was amazed by this wonder. She smiled happily at the Soaring Seagull, her eyes did not show fear, only amusement.

The elves were jumping around her and cuddling up to her. The child plopped down so the small creatures could reach her better. She then lay down, and the happily chattering elves were jumping on her. She gazed into the sun, the rocks were singing. The little girl laughed in abundance as the tiny feet tickled her body. She felt the beating marks on her body healing. The blue and green bruises disappeared under the small footsteps. This is how the Enchanted Mountain's elves cure with love and peace.

The Soaring Seagull and the Bull were ecstatic to see the little girl's joy as she lay happily among the army of elves, who were curing her. The Bull came to pick me up, the grown-up, so I could meet the little girl at the Enchanted Mountain.

By the time the Bull arrived, I had stopped crying. The little girl's battered body still hurt, and the loss she had suffered on the floor was tremendous when the small body was attacked by the predators. I dreamed that the little girl becomes a giant, and she attacks the monsters before they can touch her. The giant attacked everyone who was ever involved in this, just as I was on the floor as a child with a split-up body. I thanked the little girl that she survived. I did not blame her for not remembering or for not stumbling to the Danube to wash her body away to a different world, where there is no hurt, no shame, and no guilt.

I hopped onto the back of the Bull, and we flew up to the sky. At the foot of the Enchanted Mountain, I saw the heartily laughing, happy little girl who was playing with the elf under the Soaring Seagull's guarded glance. I smiled happily. The little girl got up, ran towards me with the elf, and hugged me joyfully.

"Thank you for coming over again. Meet my new friends. These are the Enchanted Mountain's curing elves." She chattered. Her face was enlightened with happiness.

I teared up as I hugged her. I made her accountable for why she did not jump into the water on that spring day. She was an innocent child. I kept hugging her happily for being alive, for her happiness, and for not feeling any pain. I held her tight, she is my most precious darling.

"Tell a story, tell a story, and tell my story." She asked me as she sat on the ground. The elf surrounded her. The Soaring Seagull, the Bull, and I sat down in a circle, and I started to tell the story.

The clean laundry is drying outside; the wind and the sun dry them. The kitchen is clean, and we prepare delicious food and goodies in there for our kids and for ourselves. There is no mess, dirt, or hunger. No one is cold. The Bull helped out – I looked at him gratefully. "Thank you, little girl, for all this, as this is exactly how it will be. And as you can see, we are here together."

"Thank you for telling me this. Thank you for being here with me." Her eyes showed gratefulness.

We set off to the Enchanted Mountain. The Soaring Seagull hugged the little girl and I, the Bull walked behind us. We were climbing higher and higher on the mountain. We did not get tired. We were floating as the elves were hopping around us.

Enchanted Mountain

Dance

The quiet swish of the Soaring Seagull's dress did not wake the sleeping child. Her ageless face was beaming with light as she stepped to the side of the bed. She stroked the little girl's face, which looked old from having the burden to deal with grown-up difficulties.

"Wake up, wake up. We have to go to play." She said quietly, her ageless face smiling, the little girl woke up and snuggled up to her. She dressed up and sat in the Soaring Seagull's lap. She did not say anything. She snuggled up to her very close so she could feel the warmness of a mother's hug. The Bull puffed happily and bounced around the little girl. She laughed heartily at the Bull's silliness, clapping happily. Then she slid out from the hug and started to bounce around too, pretending to be a Bull.

Then the Bull stopped. It was time to go. The Soaring Seagull put the little girl into her lap, the Bull stomped and jumped, and they flew into the starry heaven in amazement, gazing at the endless space.

"We are going to see the Angels today. Their choir and dance are waiting for you." Whispered the Soaring Seagull to the happy child.

The little girl happily snuggled up to the Soaring Seagull and waited for the amusement and wonders. The Bull stopped in front of a gate. The gate opened, and wonderful music and singing could be heard. The Angles' choir was singing. In front of the choir, many Angels were dancing the dance of the light. They were shinning like stars.

The little girl got off the back of the Bull and walked closer. She wanted to have her own light too, so she tried to catch it. She needed this light to have it in the dark, so she can live.

"Little one," called the Soaring Seagull, "You can dance with the Angels. They are waiting for you." The little girl was surprised to hear this.

The Angels were pure and bright. She stared at them with amazement.

"Come and dance with us." One Angel called her and pulled the little girl into the light by reaching for her hand.

As she danced among the Angels, the little girl felt that her body slowly filled up with light.

She was astonished to feel lighter and lighter and felt that she was flying, soaring. In a flood of lights, she imitated the Angels, and she felt that she had wings.

The Bull came to pick me up, the Adult, so I could also see the little girl in the flood of light. I was wrapped in a gloomy, dark shadow, my walking was heavy, and I felt broken. It took me a long time to walk through the gate. The Souring Seagull was waiting for me, the Universe shone through her blazing brown eyes. She loves me. We hugged each other, and I stared at the shinning little girl in amazement. She was dancing freely and lightly to the beat of the heavenly music along with the Angels. The Soaring Seagull smiled at me and whispered in my ear,

"You can join in. You can dance with the little girl and the Angels in the flood of light, but not the dance of rage, but the dance of joy and light."

Happily, I joined the Angels. The little girl hugged me kindly, and we were dancing together in the flood of light.

The Soaring Seagull and the Bull joined in, and we sang together. The light spread all around us.

Banish the shadow. Bring beautiful dreams. Memory must stay forever. Light, light, never-ending light.

Slowly, the music and the singing stopped as the flood of light ended. We started back to the infinite space. I hugged the little girl very tightly. The Soaring Seagull sat behind us on the back of the Bull. We were travelling in a night sky filled with light and joy. We were shinning just like the stars.

Dance

Jewel

"Wake up, little girl. We have to go, dear." Said the Soaring Seagull to the sleeping child. The little girl hugged her with her teary eyes and said,

"Protect me, protect me, Soaring Seagull. Hug me tight and let me feel the hug of a real mother." The Soaring Seagull warmly hugged the tiny sobbing body and said, "Don't cry, my sweet soul. I am always here with you, and the Angels are guarding you."

When the Bull showed up, the little girl got very happy. She ran towards him and patted him.

"Oh dear Bull, please don't ever leave me. Follow me and guard me all the time. It is very hard for me." She whispered into his ear.

"I will guard you, don't be scared. I will be with you all the time. Just think of me and I will be there to help you." The Bull replied quietly.

The little girl stopped crying, and a smile showed through her teary eyes. The Soaring Seagull held her hand, and they sat on the back of the Bull together. The heavenly journey started out as the stars and the moon guided their steps.

The Bull stopped in a large meadow with many sweet-scented flowers. The little girl was happily running around in the meadow and smelling the fragrant flowers. The Soaring Seagull followed her with the Bull.

Then, they all sat in the grass, and the Soaring Seagull weaved a beautiful wreath from the heavenly flowers and a garland from dewdrops. The little girl was mesmerised.

"Are these mine?" She asked doubtfully.

"Yes, they are for you, my sweet child. I made them for you." The Soaring Seagull stroked the child.

The Bull made her a pair of earrings from green grass. The little girl happily put on all the jewels. She was dancing joyfully, thinking that one day she would be a grown-up and will have real jewellery. The Bull came to get me, and I joined him happily because I knew that the little girl was fine. Many people looked after both of us and we would not be hurt.

I saw myself as a little girl in the meadow. She was shining happily in her jewellery. The sunshine reflected a million colours from her dewdrop necklace.

She ran towards me, hugged me, and we were happy in this eternal peace. The Soaring Seagull made some jewellery for me too. I was ecstatic when I put them on myself, and we were shining together —the little girl and me, the grown-up — the way real women shine.

Jewel

Golden threads

"Dear Soaring Seagull, please help me. I'm completely lost," I called out to my heavenly mother who loves me unconditionally. "I'm 50 years old and I still call her when I am stressed."

The Soaring Seagull came over to hug me, and everything got brighter all of a sudden. The Bull turned up, and we headed out to see the little girl.

"She is still asleep." Whispered the Soaring Seagull as she was stroking the sleeping child. On the floor around her bed, we saw shiny and colourful light threads. The Soaring Seagull picked all of them up and put them in her pocket.

"What are those?" I asked, surprised.

The Soaring Seagull did not answer but smiled mysteriously. "Wake up, little girl, we have to go." Said the Soaring Seagull.

The little girl woke up and snuggled up to the Soaring Seagull. I hugged her too. She was very bony. I could feel her ribs. The Bull stepped closer and asked us to pat him. We all comforted her, and we all were happy. The little girl was smiling. Her eyes did not show fear, she was not scared. She did not have to stand on guard, waiting for the next unexpected dreadful attack. She did not have to watch every move, wondering when the horror would start, the pushing, and the beating from which she was unable to protect herself.

We headed out into the sparkling night on the back of the Bull. In front of us was the endless sky. The stars were glowing, and the Angels were waiting for us.

The Bull stopped, and we got off his back. We arrived at the Heavenly Gate. All three of us were holding hands, with the little girl in the middle. She was jumping around happily, being silly. The Golden Threads were glittering in the Angels' hands. They were rolling these threads from the light of the stars, forming them into a ball. They worked quickly and sang quietly in eternal peace. The little girl walked over to them, and the light of the golden thread shone upon her.

"I am like gold!" she sang loudly and carelessly, jumping around in the golden light.

The Angels were stroking her tiny body.

The Soaring Seagull pulled out the Golden Threads from her pocket and handed them to the Angels. They held them and stroked them, knowing exactly what they were. They had seen this many times before. These were pieces of a broken soul, torn out from the little girl.

"Stitch them up nicely with Golden Threads, the way only you know how," said the Soaring Seagull to the Angels. "Make it whole again. These pieces were broken in drunken beatings and screaming."

The Angels got to work and mended the broken light threads with Golden Threads. The little girl stared at their diligent work while the Soaring Seagull sang with a smile. "Heal, heal broken souls, and let the ripped pieces be whole again. The Angels will provide the Golden Threads."

And they mended the ripped parts together.

The broken light threads became a colourful, glittery globe when the Angels finished stitching it up with the golden threads. The little girl thought it was a ball, and she threw it and bounced it happily. It was completely hers. The Bull played with her peacefully up in the sky.

The Soaring Seagull hugged me, the grown-up, and we smiled as we stared at the flying glitter-globe, which was mended by the Golden Threads. The Angels surrounded us, and we danced the dance of Angels.

The little girl got tired from playing, and she came to dance with us. The colourful glitter-globe was hovering in the middle and then disappeared.

The Soaring Seagull smiled and hugged me.

You have received what was lost long ago. The Angels mended it with golden threads and now it is yours.

I felt how my soul, my heart, and my body filled up with light and colour, and I was reborn. Happily, I hugged the little girl.

My sweet darling, thank you for everything. I will take care of you.

Then I turned to the Angels with grace and love, and said, "Thank you very much that you mended the pieces with the Golden Threads, I did not know how to do this. I am not an Angel; I am mortal, fallible."

"Well, anyone who can find the way to us with faith, can mend the pieces with the Golden Threads to show the way how to heal." Responded the Angels.

The little girl, the Soaring Seagull, the Bull, and I stood in a circle. As the Golden Threads were weaving around us, we were listening to soft music and dancing the dance of the Angels.

Golden Threads

The Gift

The Soaring Seagull's white, swishy dress was glowing as she stopped beside my bed. The Bull turned up too. I, the grown-up, stood up with teary eyes and snuggled into the Soaring Seagull's hugging arms. I was in my nightgown, crying and crying as I was in pain. And I let it hurt, because if I let it hurt, it will go away and not make me sick.

"Soaring Seagull, hug me, please. Love me, I am alone, no one loves me. I don't have any man in my life to hug me. I would like to love a man, not to hurt him but to respect him, to take care of him, and to be his true partner." I said and put my teary face on her shoulder.

"My dear sweetheart, I love you so much," whispered the Soaring Seagull. "I always will love you. Love is the strongest energy in the Universe. If you do not have a man beside you in your earthly life, the love is still yours. I will take you and show you the way. You just need to follow it. Your actions will show who you are in your earthly existence. You will please a man, and he will do the same."

The Bull was pacing around us and asked for a stroke. I patted him and hugged him, pressing my teary face to his fur. He gave me strength and I accepted it.

I received hurtful words from men that if a woman acts like a man, it doesn't make her a man nor makes her a woman. That is not natural, nor useful. I was told I don't respect the rules of nature, as I don't accept the qualities of a man from others, only from myself. Nature has many rules, but the most important is to know how to survive. This is the biggest order in this earthly life.

And if the abused, raped little girl could survive and create the way, then that is fine.

"Let's go see the little girl." Said the Soaring Seagull.

I hopped onto the back of the Bull, and the heavenly soaring started into the mist of the stars. I showed my teary face to the stars, to take my tears far away. I am going to love it.

We entered the little girl's room. She had a restless sleep. She had nightmares. The dark devils picked her and her mother up and took them away in the dark, starless night. The little girl was alone, shaken. No one was around to protect her.

"Little girl, wake up. We are going to see the Heavenly Stars." The Soaring Seagull stroked the sleeping child's face.

The little girl woke up, her face still carrying the trauma of the nightmare, yet happily jumped into the embrace of the Soaring Seagull. When she saw me, she hugged me and the Bull too. She was happy.

"Thank you for coming over to see me." She whispered, tears of joy streaming down her face. I hugged her and gently rocked her. She asked me to tell her a story, but this time I could not tell her a nice story.

"Little girl, there is a lot of pain in earthly existence. And I know, dear, that you had a lot of pain, and you have ignored it to survive. As a grown-up, I have done the same. I did not see any other way to deal with it. Only rarely do I let my pain touch me. But now, it is here, and I will cry for you and for myself too. But remember, there is also happiness, peace, calmness, beautiful memories, dreams, presents, healing, and acceptance, not just pain."

"You know, little girl, so many people saw me as a strong woman who could solve everything. I would laugh it off, of course, but I could not show my pain. I could not show how tired and hurt I was, how thousands of small needles jabbed into me, inflaming my skin. I ignored all of them, clenched my teeth, and carried on. I tolerated everything, even from my husband, whom I loved and who loved me too, yet we hurt each other a lot. Even then, I continued to chase after others, always putting them before myself. But I promise you, little girl, this time you will be the most important. My gift to you is that I will heal you. And perhaps I never will have a partner, a man beside me, and I will not have love, romance, peace, or calm in togetherness. However, we will still be together in peace, along with the Soaring Seagull and the Bull. They will help us as long as the Universe continues to show its wonders. I am grateful for my life."

This is how we were rocked together in peace. We are alive, we are in peace and it is calm. The Soaring Seagull, the Bull, the Universe, and the Creator are guarding us. Let their will be done.

The Gift

A man is being born

The Soaring Seagull was gently stroking the little boy. She smiled lovingly. The little boy could feel this in his dream.

"Wake up, wake up." She called out.

The little boy woke up and was amazed by the Soaring Seagull's smile. It was so inviting that he got into her lap right away and embraced her.

"I love you very much, the way you are. I know that your earthly mother always tells you that she wished you were born as a girl. Little boy, you will be a man. You are not a girl. I will help you, as I am your heavenly mother."

The little boy was smiling happily in her embrace, knowing that finally, he can be who he is and not someone else.

The Bull arrived, and the little boy was patting him joyfully.

"Let's go, little boy. We have to meet someone and we have to play." Said the Soaring Seagull.

The little boy got dressed, and all of them set out to fly into the sky to reach the stars on the back of the Bull. They stopped at the edge of the Heavenly River, where heavenly trees were bending and swaying on the shore. The little boy waded into the water, and no one reprimanded him. It was allowed to be in there. He felt the rushing water on his skin while the Soaring Seagull smilingly watched the playing child.

The Bull comes for me, the grown-up. I am tired and sad. My life has fallen apart. I am living with my older son, who is not well, and neither am I. My partner cheated on me many times, and I knew it and tolerated it. She was the love of my life, and I was not able to leave her. It took me great effort to do it. I felt weak when I was with her.

As the Bull stopped beside my bed, I set on his back. He said there is someone important I must meet.

We were soaring into the sky, up to the stars, and we reached the Heavenly River. The Soaring Seagull's hug was waiting for me. The Universe glazed from her blazing brown eyes. She radiated love, and I was happy to hug her. She loved me for who I was.

When the little boy saw me, he ran out from the Heavenly River and hugged me.

"Am I going to be this big and strong when I grow up? That will be so great." He said joyfully.

I hugged him too, and we were rocking together, the little boy and me, with the Soaring Seagull. The Bull was walking around us. We were in a protective circle. I finally felt at home. I always will visit the little boy so we can recover together, and will become the man I want to be without any judgements.

A man is being born

At the Natives

The little boy was in his bed. He was restless and could not sleep well, as his five-year-old body was aching from the work he had to do. He had to wake up at daybreak to go to the cornfield to harvest the corn. His father constantly told him to keep working to grow into a strong and tough man.

After day-care in the afternoon, he had to deal with the chickens, had to pluck and clean them until darkness.

His younger brother played in his mother's lap inside the house. The little boy worked outside. The Soaring Seagull was beaming in her white dress. She stepped to the side of his bed and whispered,

"Wake up, little boy. We will go to play."

The Bull arrived too. The little boy's stare was drowsy.

"Are you taking me to play, indeed?" He asked happily.

He got dressed fast and hopped onto the back of the Bull. The Bull playfully danced. The little boy giggled and held on tight.

"Gee, wee! I am the strongest!" He exclaimed joyfully on the back of the Bull.

The Soaring Seagull enjoyed seeing the little boy to be strong and smart. She sat behind the little boy on the back of the Bull. He happily snuggled into her embrace and felt right at home.

The Bull was soaring, flying up into the sky. The little boy tried to catch the stars. He shouted to the Bull, "Go higher, go higher!" The Soaring Seagull kept laughing.

"We are flying higher and higher, and you can conquer the starry sky." The Bull whispered, and the little boy was nodding.

The Bull kept flying but knew that one day he would be his master. The little boy would grow up and be stronger than him, but until then, he must protect him from harm.

The Soaring Seagull was hugging the little boy in eternal love, to make the sadness leave his little heart and the darkness disappear so that the healing light of unconditional love could shine forever. The Bull stopped at the edge of a huge forest. They heard music, people talking, and dogs barking. The little boy got very curious and ran ahead, followed by the Bull.

He saw a native camp. He was mesmerised by it, as he had never seen this in real life, only in pictures. The children called him to play with them. They played at being hunters, learning how to step silently so the wildlife would not be alarmed. The little boy joyfully played along. He tried the archery too. The Soaring Seagull proudly watched how precise his shooting was. The Bull also noticed how his skills got better and better.

The Bull then came over to me, the grown-up man, who the little guy will be one day. I had been waiting for him for a long time. I knew he would come to me one day so I could meet him. The time had come. I jumped onto the back of the

Bull, and we soared and flew up high into the sky. We stopped at the Native Camp.

I saw the little boy. He was happy in the Soaring Seagull's embrace. When he noticed me, he knew who I was and happily hugged me.

"You will be me. Tell me a story about our life. Tell me my tale." He asked.

"We will be happy and will have a good life. We will have four children and a wonderful, kind, smart wife. Then we will have some storms, which will end as storms always do, and a new day will start with a new creation. This is the life of a man, and sometimes it will be difficult. Our children will not work in the fields. They will go to school, play sports, and we will provide them with everything we can." I told him.

"So, little boy, what would you like to do now?" I asked.

"I want to play a lot. Please take me to play. Here we have the Soaring Seagull, who always hugs me and loves me, and that is comforting for me. Right now, I am happy."

The Soaring Seagull and the Bull surrounded us, and I felt peace in this togetherness. I will not forget to take the little boy to play.

The little boy went back to play happily with the Natives. The Soaring Seagull hugged me, and we stayed embraced. The slender, fragile woman with her ageless face, and I, the tall strong man. Yet, she was the strong one, and I was the fragile one. But I was happy about this, as finally, I had arrived home to feel my mother's hug.

At the Natives

Love

The tiny babies were inside the small cribs, which were lined up beside each other. The babies did not cry, as no one would hear them anyway. Only two nannies were to look after them, and they could not keep up.

The babies already knew that they would not be picked up even if they cried. The babies were silent. Life did not bring sweet music into this room. The little babies were dreaming about a place where they could be rocked and loved.

At midnight, the Soaring Seagull arrived in her swished white dress to hug the little ones. She embraced them, rocked them, and stroked them so they could feel loved. She was their heavenly mother who showed them that the Universe would not let them be alone. She knew that there are good people who come in to rock the little babies so they can feel the touch of the strokes on their skin. The Bull dropped by. The tiny hands touched his fur, and he was happily puffing between the little cribs. The windows opened, and an army of Angels flew right into the room. The Soaring Seagull was smiling happily as the Angels flew around her slender body, and then each flew over a crib to guard a baby. They would be the guardian angels. They would guard the abandoned.

As the quiet heavenly music was playing, the babies started to gurgle. They had voices too, but not everyone could hear them. Now the Angels, the Soaring Seagull, and the Bull could hear them. This brought peace to the place.

The love, as the Golden Thread, was swimming in the air. The little babies tried to reach them with their tiny hands. They tried to touch the Golden Threads. The Golden Threads were twisting and flying between them, until the entire room got covered with it, while the music was playing and the babies were dreaming.

Every night, they were dreaming beautiful dreams so they could be able to live in peace and love under their guardian angels' protection.

Love

Star Powder

"Dream beautiful dreams, little girl. Dream that I love you." The Soaring Seagull whispered. The little girl tossed and turned in her bed, and then opened her eyes. She snuggled up to the Soaring Seagull where she had no harm, scare, pain or madness, but only love.

"No one loves me, I am scared," whispered the little girl. "I am scared to talk, I am a coward. They don't even notice me, I am invisible. I am scared of everyone. Soaring Seagull, please help me."

"I love you little one, I love you the way you are." The Soaring Seagull embraced and rocked the little girl so she would not be scared anymore and would not feel the pain of the maze of life, she was thrown into too early.

The Bull arrived and watched them embrace each other. He knew that the little girl broke emotionally from the pain.

The Bull came to pick up the grown-up, me, the grown-up who the little girl would be. I watched with amazement how the tormented little girl of shame and guilt was comforted in the Soaring Seagull's lap. The Soaring Seagull reached for me and hugged me as well.

"Little girl, little girl, I remember you. You were scared to talk, you hid away, and you played that you were invisible.

There was a lot of fighting at home and you hid as you were scared." I was hugging the child, who I once was. "I love you, sweet little one, for me you are the most important. I will heal you and I will recover too. Soaring Seagull, please help us."

The Soaring Seagull embraced us both and we cried. It was painful to be so alone and that we were not able to talk. Neither the little girl nor the grown-up. As a grown-up, I am still scared, I didn't dare to talk as I was still flooded with shame and guilt.

The Bull walked up to us and asked for a stroke. After that, we all hopped onto his back and started our heavenly flight. Our tears dried by the light of the stars and the moon.

Up high in the sky on the back of the flying Bull, the Soaring Seagull embraced the little girl and me, as we marvelled at all the wonders around us.

The Bull stopped on one star. The Earth was very far. The star shined and gave out a warm light. We all stood there, glowing in the Soaring Seagull's embrace. The Bull lay on the star and started to wiggle. His fur had star powder all over.

The golden and glowing star powder sprinkled on us. We laughed and jumped joyfully in it.

The Soaring Seagull happily watched our joy in the glow. She came closer to us and sang softly,

Little girl and the grown-up
Remember, that you took a bath in star powder
Heavenly parents
We love you
There is no shame and guilt in this world
Talk, feel and trust!

And as the singing kept going in the star powder, I promised the little girl that I was not going to be invisible anymore. I, as a grown-up, was not going to hide anymore and would not be scared. My heavenly parents were with me all the time. I would let the little girl be happy and without any fear. She was my most precious gift.

Star Powder

The pain

The little boy laid in his bed down-heartedly. His small body was beaten by a belt. His father was drunk again. He did not have tears anymore as boys don't cry – his father screamed this all the time.

Soaring Seagull's white dress swished in the room and she stepped to the little boy's bed. She stroked his tired face.

"Little boy wake up. We need to go because the forest is waiting"– she whispered.

Little boy opened his eyes and looked around in amazement. Soaring Seagull's blazing brown eyes calmed him as she embraced him with her hug.

"Thank you for being here. I was waiting for you so much"– he whispered to Soaring Seagull.

The Bull arrived and the little boy ran to him.

"I have already seen you, I met you before"– and he petted him happily.

He got dressed fast and set on the back of the Bull with Soaring Seagull. The heavenly ride started between the stars. The little boy was laughing with joy in the embrace of Soaring Seagull.

Soon a heavenly road opened up and they could see the Heavenly Forest. The Bull stopped in a clearing. Soaring

Seagull and the little boy walked toward the Forest by holding hands. The Bull followed them by guarding their steps.

"Go on and climb up on the trees. You allowed to do that"– Soaring Seagull encouraged him. Little boy was climbing on the trees happily. The birds were chirping and fluttering around and greeted him.

The Bull came to pick me up, the grown-up. I had a hungover, my head was hurting. I was dismayed by his presence. Why would anyone be here anyway?

"Came to pick you up, someone is waiting for you. There are people who would love to meet you."– the Bull muttered into my ear.

I got dressed and sat on his back. I was surprised. No one ever wanted to meet me besides my drinking buddies.

We were Soaring in the sky. My headache disappeared, and the bright stars cleared my head. I calmed down, nothing was hunting me. I was dreaming in the dense heaven.

We stopped at the Heavenly Forest. Soaring Seagull turned toward me. Her eyes were beaming with the love of the Universe. I stepped up to her and we hugged each other. Her embrace felt like a cleansing bath. I felt right at home in the embrace of my Heavenly mother's arms. No more pain no more rut. My tears started to flow. I was ever grateful. I saw the little boy who I was as a child up on the tree between the leafy boughs. The little boy climbed off the tree and ran to me.

"You will be me, I am so happy you came over. Please tell me how life will be when I grow up, hope it will be better and no one will beat me"– he exclaimed happily.

My tears were flooding down on my face. How can I tell him that I have a drinking problem, that I am not able to be without alcohol and my life is about to find alcohol to drink to forget the pain? When I drink there is no pain.

I looked at Soaring Seagull and the Bull with entreaty asking what to do. Soaring Seagull stepped over to us, hugged us both and whispered:

"The little boy has a lot of pain which he hides. The grown-up drinks in order to flee from his pain."

The little boy cried with me in the Heavenly Forest. The Bull created a magic circle around us with his hoof in the Heavenly Clearing.

"Just cry and cry. The tears of pain will be swollen by the Heavenly clearing and there will be Heavenly flowers instead of the tears."– the Bull muttered.

My pain melted away in the embrace of Soaring Seagull. "Dear little boy, yes I drink a lot of alcohol. This is my life about right now. But I am here with you with Soaring Seagull and the Bull who were sent by the Universe. I will come and visit you again and again because for me you are the most important. I also promise little boy that I will stop drinking. Soaring Seagull and the Bull will help me in this."

And the Heavenly flowers kept growing where our tears dropped. Little boy and I were smiling gratefully as we were recovering from our pain together.

The Pain